The Garden of Love

A.D. HEWITT

First published in paperback by
Michael Terence Publishing in 2022
This edition published 2023
www.mtp.agency

Copyright © 2023 A.D. Hewitt

A.D. Hewitt has asserted the right to be identified as
the author of this work in accordance with the
Copyright, Designs and Patents Act 1988

ISBN 9781800944381

No part of this publication may be reproduced, stored
in a retrieval system, or transmitted, in any form or
by any means, electronic, mechanical, photocopying,
recording or otherwise, without the prior
permission of the publisher

Cover image
Copyright © Rostislavsedlacek
www.123rf.com

Cover design
Copyright © 2022 Michael Terence Publishing

Michael Terence
Publishing

Contents

PART ONE 1

Chapter 1: Tea at the Country House 3

Chapter 2: Spring Term 7

Chapter 3: Anthony's Misery 10

Chapter 4: Tea in the Garden 12

Chapter 5: Anthony's Personal Reflection of Angelica 16

Chapter 6: Mrs Wills Invites Guests to Tea 19

Chapter 7: Anthony Alone in the Garden 23

Chapter 8: Secrets and Fascinations 25

Chapter 9: The Portrait 28

Chapter 10: Daydreams 30

Chapter 11: Late Night Conversation 32

Chapter 12: The Mid - Afternoon Walk Out in the Garden 34

PART TWO 39

Chapter 1: Angelica's Surprise Visit (Stately Prominence) 41

Chapter 2: Anthony's Deep Reflection on Angelica 46

Chapter 3: Christmas Break 50

Chapter 4: Anthony's Brief Time Alone at Blue Orchid 52

Chapter 5: The Derby 57

Chapter 6: Midnight Love in the Garden 60

PART ONE

Chapter 1

Tea at the Country House

Yesterday, Anthony had gone to a friend's party. Once there he felt unloved and unwanted.

Today, his mother and he had been invited for tea at Mrs Dobbs'. Going out in the large garden. He was stunned by the beauty of the garden. Walking out alone in the garden he walked past people, guests strolling by. One couple held hands. He heard the sweet sound of birdsong. Suddenly a robin perched on a wooden fence and then flew away.

Anthony imagined beautiful virgins surrounding him. Coming to touch him. Their hands coming from everywhere. Was it a vision?

A handsome woman, charmingly sweet. In his fantasy, he desired all of the virgins! Not just one but all of them!

Anthony became enamoured with the virgin beauties who engaged in narcissistic exhibitionism. The sight of them took his breath away.

From his senses and sense of reality. He soon realised it was only a dream! A fantasy!

He did wish he was loved, adored and admired. In reality, he was usually spurned, shunned and unloved!

Going back indoors he re-joined his Mother and Mrs Dobbs. They sat together in the lounge and talked.

"How is school?" asked Mrs Dobbs.

"Don't ask. I am not having a good time of it. I will be glad when it's all over," replied Anthony.

"Do study. Get your exams. I can't stress enough how important it is. I must emphasise how important it is," urged Mrs Dobbs.

"I never do well at school," groaned Anthony.

"You must try. Dear boy! You are only a boy. You need to grow up," said Mrs Dobbs.

Anthony felt humiliated.

Opposite, Anthony saw straight ahead on a cabinet a silver-framed photograph of Angelica, Mrs Dobbs' Grand-daughter. Anthony admired the pretty girl with beautiful long hair and plaits. She was crushingly stunning.

Nowadays he never seemed to see Angelica. He desired her. He longed to meet her again. He would have liked to have met Angelica. Feeling disappointed again Anthony rejected his desire to meet her.

Mrs Dobbs, Mrs Wills and Anthony stood up.

"Thank you for inviting me," said Anthony appreciatively.

"Do come again. You're welcome here. Do listen to your Mother. Be good to her," said Mrs Dobbs.

"Before we go, let's take a look at your garden,"

insisted Mrs Wills.

Mrs Dobbs, Mrs Wills and her son went out in the back garden. Admiring the garden. They marvelled at the beautiful garden.

"You do have such a lovely garden," remarked Mrs Wills.

Anthony got excited at the sight of the garden. (It was the most lovely garden he had ever been in and seen.)

"I wish I could play here all day," said Anthony dreamily.

Mrs Dobbs thought of her playful Grand-Daughter.

"Angelica would like that. She loves to play," smiled Mrs Dobbs.

"Angelica didn't come," said Mrs Wills.

"She couldn't come. Angelica's too busy doing her homework. You're welcome to stay here if you like," said Mrs Dobbs politely.

Mrs Wills accepted the invitation to stay at BLUE ORCHID. Mrs Wills decided to spend the night.

"Thank you very much. We would like to stay very much," thanked Mrs Wills.

Anthony rubbed his hands together.

"Mrs Dobbs, can we?" said Anthony excitedly.

Anthony got excited about the invitation to stay at BLUE ORCHID.

Appreciating the welcome of the invitation Mrs Wills intended to do Mrs Dobbs a favour out of appreciative gratitude.

That night Anthony hoped Angelica would come tonight. But Angelica did not come that night. Anthony became lost in his deep romantic fantasies! He became disappointed at Angelica's absence!

The next day Mrs Wills and her son set off on a long journey to drive back home.

As soon as Anthony reached home, he went into his bedroom. His Mother came into his bedroom. Paying heed to her son.

"You had a good time. It's a shame you didn't see Angelica," said Mother.

Anthony wondered. "Why didn't she come?" groaned Anthony.

"Maybe Angelica had things to do," answered Mother.

"Mrs Dobbs says Angelica loves her dresses. That Angelica wears a new dress every day," said Anthony.

"Angelica looks pretty in dresses," remarked Mother.

Anthony waved his hand in disapproving objection.

"Too pretty for my liking," sighed Anthony.

Anthony's Mother left her son's bedroom. Feeling tired, lethargic and sleepy. Anthony slumped on an armchair then within minutes he dozed off.

Tonight there was a full moon.

Chapter 2

Spring Term

Anthony sat at the front of the class in the Chemistry room. During the lesson, Anthony sitting on a stool dozed off while the class did an experiment for their practical.

The Chemistry Teacher using a chalk, drew diagrams on the blackboard. With the apparatus used for the experiment. This Chemistry group was good at Chemistry.

Anthony awoke during the Chemistry lesson. In his exercise book, he copied down the diagrams of the experiment. He had little interest in this experiment or the subject.

After the Chemistry lesson had ended. It was break-time.

Going on the school grounds he looked for any of the ones, female pupils he desired, but none of them took any interest in him. Anthony felt miserable and quite unhappy. He did dread taking his Examinations in the Summer Term. He knew he would fail his Examinations without doubt. He was destined to fail. (In some of his subjects Anthony was in the bottom sets. During private entry, he did change sets. He was transferred to the top sets in two of his subjects.)

These are his favourite subjects.

Anthony went to the Tuck Shop. There he queued up at the Tuck Shop. He desired a lovely-looking schoolgirl. The schoolgirl showed no interest in him. The Fifth Year pupil undesired the schoolboy.

At the Tuck Shop. He bought a can of Coke and a packet of crisps. After the bell sounded Anthony attended his English lesson. The Teacher emphasised the set should practise writing Essays in the allocated time set under Examination conditions. It would be against the clock. During the lesson, the set did spend their time writing an essay. This essay. (The composition from a past Examination paper.) Anthony did write but did not reach the standard of a pass. (In the previous English lesson the Head of English did emphasise in composition that FACTUAL concluded Paper 1.)

During lunchtime, Anthony played Football in the playground for a short time.

Later Anthony attended Registration. Most of the Form was present. There was absenteeism at Registration. After registration Anthony attended his History lesson in the History block.

During the History lesson, the class did dictation which was done by the Teacher. The Pupils wrote down everything the Teacher dictated. The Second World War History.

After the lesson had ended, Anthony had gone back to his Form room with his Form present.

Leaving school and going home, Anthony had no

wish to attend school for the next few days.

Anthony lost interest in doing revision and attending revision classes.

Anthony skived off school.

The next term was the Summer Term. There were EXAMINATIONS at the start of the Summer Term.

Anthony a candidate failed his exams!

Chapter 3

Anthony's Misery

Anthony stayed at home. His Mother remained at home. Mrs Wills still hadn't gone to work yet. Sitting on the armchair, Anthony spent time doing his revision. He revised History. Mrs Wills burst into the room. Mrs Wills agitated her son for being at home. Staying at home. The absentee took liberties.

"Shouldn't you be at school? You won't pass," said Mother assuredly.

Anthony humiliated. "Yes. Mom. I won't."

"Son. I do worry about you," said Mother worriedly.

Anthony worried about his life. The worrier tensed up.

"All I can do is my best. No one loves me," said Anthony miserably.

"Son. You will find someone nice. I assure you," undoubted Mother.

"But who?" shrugged Anthony.

"I don't know exactly. You will find someone."

"I just can't see it," doubted Anthony. "How can I be loved? Who will love me?"

"You shouldn't doubt. You shouldn't worry."

Anthony wondered who would love him.

He was unamused at his fantasy. Usually, with his fantasies he had ecstasies.

Anthony felt sorry for himself.

"Who would date me? Who would marry me? I am unmarriable and undesirable."

"Angelica would," smirked Mother.

"Are you a matchmaker? Don't make fun of me. Don't be ridiculous!"

Anthony was tearful and deeply unhappy. He got up from the armchair and rushed out of the room. He went upstairs to his bedroom. He ran and threw himself down on his bed. He began to cry. On a table was an open book of gardens of photography of really beautiful gardens and photographed natural landscapes.

Chapter 4

Tea in the Garden

Mrs Wills and her son came to Blue Orchid for tea.

Earlier in the afternoon, Mrs Dobbs showed Mrs Wills and Anthony her Art in her house. They both looked at the paintings, pictures and portraits. One of the portraits was of Mrs Dobbs' Great-Grandmother. They both took pleasure from their privilege.

Mrs Dobbs did not explain her Art collection. It remained confidential and it was her obsessive interest. It was an obsessional occupation. Her Husband was an Art collector.

Later they had tea in the garden. They sat out in the shade. The blazing sun shone.

"Young man. What do you want to do as a profession?" asked Mrs Dobbs.

"I want to be a writer," replied Anthony.

"That's a hard job. Best of luck with your endeavour. You do have a good imagination. You're artistic. Aren't you?" said Mrs Dobbs admiringly.

"Where is Angelica?" asked Anthony.

"I must apologise. I am afraid Angelica could not make it. It's a shame," said Mrs Dobbs disappointedly.

The Garden of Love

Anthony was disappointed at Angelica not coming to tea today this afternoon. Angelica declined her invitation to tea. Anthony remained too disappointed. He did look forward to meeting Angelica again. Mrs Wills and Mrs Dobbs talked while Anthony kept silent. He was too upset. Anthony's high expectations were a disappointment. An unfulfillment. Anthony did not want to stay long at BLUE ORCHID. He really wanted to go home. Anthony felt disconcerted. He did not listen to the ladies' conversation.

Anthony got up from the garden chair. Going in a direction, he wandered down the garden alone. He was amazed at the lovely garden. In summer the large country garden was beautiful. It had the loveliest trees. The rose garden bloomed with roses. He was stunned at the breath-taking sight of all the beautiful roses everywhere. He smelled the scent of the glorious roses. The rose scent was an exquisiteness of natural gloriousness.

Leaving the country house, Anthony and his Mother went to a car parked in a stone ground drive. They both got in the car. Mrs Wills stood by the doorway. Waving goodbye to them. Mrs Wills' emotion was passionate.

Anthony had no wish to return to BLUE ORCHID. His unfulfilled dream was a disappointment! His desire for Angelica was an infatuation.

He hated Angelica! Yet he still loved her. Did he remain ambivalent towards Angelica? One of the eldest Grandchildren. One of the Grand-Daughters.

About an hour later the car reached their home.

At home, late at night, Anthony rested on the settee. His Mother brought her son a glass of fresh milk and cookies. In a dreamy state. He relaxed. Resting in comfort. Anthony had been lethargic, lackadaisical and sleepy.

"Well. Son. What did you think of Blue Orchid?" asked Mother.

"It's a lovely place. It has a wonderful garden. You could fall in love there. It's romantic," answered Anthony.

"It's a pity. We didn't stay long," murmured Mother.

"What are visitors for?" moaned son.

"It's a shame. You didn't see Angelica."

Anthony got deeply upset about Angelica's absence. He felt rather unhappy and deeply sad.

"Why didn't Angelica come?"

Anthony's parent defended Angelica's absence.

"Maybe Angelica has other things to do?"

Anthony expressed his feeling.

"Angelica dislikes me. I know it. I am not going there again," grumbled Son.

The parent tried to comfort her son.

"How can you not? Isn't it a lovely place?"

In anger, Anthony protested.

"Why didn't Angelica come? I was expecting her for

tea. She didn't come. Why not?"

"Angelica is a rich Grand-daughter. She must have her reasons," said Mother.

Anthony expostulated. "Is Angelica justified? Certainly not. Angelica did not turn up for tea. Why didn't she? I won't go there again. I never will," sulked Son.

Anthony had such a tantrum. He got up from the settee. Leaving his tired Mother all alone downstairs.

Anthony came out of the lounge. He was sleepy. He could not stay awake any longer. He went upstairs. The light was bright. He went to his bedroom. He went to bed. At that time it was a few minutes past midnight. Anthony fell asleep in bed. Anthony a sad boy dreamt of paradise!

Chapter 5

Anthony's Personal Reflection of Angelica

Anthony sat down on the armchair. He began to read a comic. At once he was disturbed when his Mother came into the room. His Mother sat down on the armchair opposite. They both sat facing each other. His Mother intruded on him. She invaded his privacy. The son objected to his Mother's intrusion. He was irritated.

"Have you been crying?" asked Mother.

"Me! No! Don't," muttered Son.

"What are you reading?"

"I am reading the Mysterious Master of Ceremonies," replied Son.

"That's mystical. You are not still down about Angelica."

Anthony admitted to the way he felt with regard to Angelica.

"I am still down. Why does she not like me? Why doesn't Angelica join me for tea?" grumbled Son.

"Don't take it to heart. Angelica could not come,"

defended Mother.

The son spoke in a sardonic tone of voice. "Excuses. Why couldn't Angelica have come?"

"Luv. I don't know."

"Why didn't Angelica come? She should have come," said Son miserably.

"Son. I don't know. Your guess is as good as mine."

"I have no intention of going there again," objected Son.

"Mrs Wills is a nice woman. We shouldn't disappoint her."

"Angelica puts on her lovely dress. She doesn't want to get it ruined."

"Angelica is pampered. She wears pretty dresses," remarked Mother.

"I wore my Sunday best. My best clothes. What was it for? Was it worth it?"

"Son. You looked smart. My good-looking son."

Anthony fantasised a dream. He took pleasure from daydreaming. A fantasy romance he imagined in his daydream.

"Will I ever be with Angelica?" wished Anthony.

"Son. I am sure you will."

Anthony doubted his fantasy dream!

"I doubt if I will ever be with Angelica."

"Why do you doubt? Be positive. Angelica might come to Mrs Wills' house."

"I don't know. I wish it will happen."

His Mother got up from the armchair. The parent neglected her son and attended to her Daughter instead. Anthony engaged in his romantic fantasies. He fully realised it was only a fantasy. From being unexcited he lost interest in it.

Anthony finished reading a comic. In his dreams, he dreamt of Angelica. He did wish he fell in love with her!

Chapter 6

Mrs Wills Invites Guests to Tea

Anthony and his Mother were invited to tea at Mrs Wills' country house. To Anthony's surprise, Angelica had been invited to tea as well.

Anthony and his Mother, Mrs Wills and Angelica sat at the garden table. They had tea together. Today the weather was fine. A glorious sunny day.

Anthony perked up. He was on his best behaviour. He had been smitten with the lovely dressed girl.

Anthony wondered why Angelica came to tea. What made Angelica come? Angelica had declined the last invitation to tea at Mrs Wills'. Mrs Wills insisted that Angelica came next time.

Anthony had a smirk. He desired Angelica an elegant Grand-Daughter. He had been overwhelmed. He did not talk to her. He was shy and diffident. What was Angelica's impression of Anthony? He did not make much of an impression.

Anthony was very happy Angelica came to tea. Angelica was intelligent, sophisticated and cosmopolitan.

After having tea Mrs Wills and Mrs Dobbs talked. Both Anthony and Angelica got up and left the garden table. They had been excused.

"Shall we go for a walk?" smiled Angelica.

"Yes. I would like that," said Anthony excitedly.

Both Anthony and Angelica walked around the country garden. Admiring the lovely garden. Marvelling at its beauty.

Anthony enjoyed her company. He was overwhelmed at her presence. Walking alongside her. Desiring to impress her. With wonder they exclaimed.

"It's lovely here," marvelled Angelica.

"So. It is. It's lovely here. Isn't it a lovely day?"

"It is. Truly marvellous."

"Why did you come?" asked Anthony.

"My Aunt told me off. I had let everyone down. I did have my problems."

Anthony did relish the garden tea. He did enjoy it immensely, especially in the dream garden.

With joy, Anthony expressed his heartfelt appreciation.

"I am glad you've come. You have made my day. Will we see each other again?"

"Perhaps. I don't know when. Crikey! I must go."

Angelica glanced at her wristwatch. Angelica became impatient. Angelica walked away from Anthony.

Going towards the direction of the country house.

Angelica departed. Angelica had been picked up by her Father and driven home.

Anthony was bewildered at Angelica's sudden departure.

Anthony avoided Mrs Wills and his Mother. He was quite upset when Angelica had gone. He preferred to be all alone now. He thought of Angelica. Desiring the English girl.

He wondered if he would ever meet Angelica again.

Angelica's departure made Anthony upset. It was upsetting to see her leave so soon. He cherished his moments with Angelica. He had a pleasant time with Angelica. He did have good memories of her. Spending the remaining time together with Mrs Wills and his Mother. At present Mrs Wills took the opportunity to show black and white photographs. Anthony had seen a few photographs of Angelica. He desired her. He had been attracted to her.

The lanky girl's good looks. Her rosy cheeks. An English rose!

After they had relaxation in a conservatory. Mrs Dobbs decided to leave BLUE ORCHID now. Mrs Dobbs drove home. A country drive back home. With such scenic charm!

Reaching home Son and Mother spent time together in the lounge. Anthony expressed himself.

"It was a nice day. A nice tea. We had a lovely time at Mrs Wills' house. I enjoyed meeting Angelica. When will we meet again? I wish I could see Angelica again!"

Chapter 7

Anthony Alone in the Garden

On a Saturday afternoon, Anthony sat out in the garden. He stayed outside for a long time. His Mother came out into the garden. Mrs Dobbs brought her son a glass of orange squash. Anthony appreciated his thoughtful Mother. He took a glass of orange squash from his Mother. He gulped it down. Quenching his thirst.

Somewhere at the back of the garden. They sat down on garden chairs in the shade. There it was cooler in the shade there in that shady spot in the garden.

"Son. Are you alright?" asked Mother.

"Yes. Mother," replied Son.

"Isn't it hot," exclaimed Mother.

"Yeah too hot."

"You're not still thinking of Angelica. Are you?"

Anthony responded in response to his Mother's perception.

"I am thinking of Angelica. My heart breaks. I shall never see her."

"I am positive you will see her. Why shouldn't you? When I don't know," assured Mother.

"What do you know about Angelica?"

"Angelica comes from a wealthy family. Her Father is a businessman and his Mother is a businesswoman. Angelica loves Art, horses and music. She's got a cat. She once went to a London Grammar School," answered Mother.

"Angelica doesn't talk much about herself. She keeps away from me. I don't really see her much."

"You poor boy! Don't see Angelica. I shall love you and leave you. I have got things to do," cuddled Mother.

Mrs Dobbs took the empty glass. Leaving her son alone. Mrs Dobbs walked back to the house. Mrs Dobbs going indoors.

Preferring to be alone. Anthony contemplated. He was meditative.

"If Angelica went away. My heart would break!"

Anthony dreamed of Angelica. A romantic daydream. Then realising it was reality. Anthony felt saddened at not seeing Angelica. He longed to see her. He yearned for her. In the cool shade, Anthony cooled down. He stayed out in the garden. He engaged in deep contemplation. His deep thoughts made him deeply upset and sad. Going back into the house. He stayed indoors.

Chapter 8

Secrets and Fascinations

Anthony stayed downstairs. Tonight. He stayed up late at night. Alone by himself, Anthony thought of Angelica.

His sister Jane arrived home. Jane came home from her friend's house. Jane came into the lounge. Jane sat down on the armchair facing her Brother who was deep in thought.

Anthony relaxed. He took comfort from being comfortable.

"I forgot to ask you. How was tea at Mrs Wills'?" gasped sister.

"It was great. I had a lovely time. Guess what. I met Angelica. Isn't that a surprise? I wasn't expecting Angelica to come. Angelica made my day by coming. Angelica looked lovely. I don't know why she even bothered to come. She hadn't come to Mrs Wills' last tea. Perhaps Mrs Wills told off Angelica. Angelica was friendly, nice and polite. We did not talk much. We had tea together. We walked together alone in the garden. It's romantic! It's a wonderful garden. I love having tea at Blue Orchid. It was even better at being in the company of Angelica. Angelica is really pretty. If you go into one of the rooms in the house there you will find portraits. A portrait of Mrs Wills, a young woman. A classy lady. Angelica does resemble Mrs Wills. They look alike," explained Brother.

Jane seemed quite astonished.

"Does she really!"

Anthony was stunned in astonishment.

"It's amazing. She does."

"Did you find out anything else? Any secrets?" wondered sister.

Anthony explained his finding.

"The thing that I found out is that Angelica looks like Mrs Wills. According to the portrait, they both look alike. Isn't it a coincidence!"

"Well, that's something!" murmured sister.

"Mrs Wills' Husband collects Art. He's an Art dealer."

"Oh! Is he? How wonderful."

"They collect Art and Antiques."

"How interesting. Do you like Angelica?"

"Yes. I do. I guess I do. I do like her."

Anthony was ashamed to admit his crush on Angelica. So he preferred to stay quiet about being besotted about her. Did an enamoured Anthony have an infatuation for Angelica? An obsessive love for her.

"This Angelica will break your heart," warned sister.

"I hope not. I wish she won't."

"It's late. I am going to bed. Goodnight!" yawned sister.

Jane left the dimly lit lounge to go to bed. Anthony stayed downstairs in the room. He remained comfortable. Sitting on the armchair. He dozed off. That night Anthony dreamt! He had a strange dream!

In a beautiful country garden there the happy and joyful children played together. Running around in great excitement. One of the playful children playing was Angelica, a ghost!

Anthony dreamt this dream.

Chapter 9

The Portrait

Arriving at Blue Orchid Mrs Wills welcomed Mrs Dobbs and her son. To Anthony's disappointment, Angelica wasn't present today for tea. Anthony stayed indoors looking at paintings and portraiture. While Mrs Dobbs and Mrs Wills came outside in the garden. They sat down at the garden table and talked.

Anthony had been occupied looking at paintings and portraiture on the walls. Going into a room. There he looked at a portrait of Mrs Wills. Angelica a Granddaughter resembled Mrs Wills' Great-Grandmother. The Grand-daughter Angelica had a striking likeness, a family resemblance.

Anthony marvelled at the portrait. He admired it. Anthony wondered at people's reaction to it. What did Guests and Visitors make of it? The portraits. The resemblance between them was a coincidence! The Great-Grandmother Victorian! Anthony shuddered. Was it haunting?

The room had antiques, furniture and a fireplace. It smelled of rich leather and polished wood. The wood was varnished.

Leaving the room. He came out of the side door into the garden. There he joined Mrs Wills and his Mother sitting out in the garden. Enjoying their relaxation.

Anthony uninterested in talking had walked off. Going alone in the garden. Walking about there. Admiring the garden. Marvelling at its beauty. He imagined Angelica in the garden. This time Angelica wasn't present. Losing interest in BLUE ORCHID and having afternoon tea later with Mrs Wills.

Anthony had never seen a country garden quite beautiful as this ever before. In the summertime, the garden had a natural gloriousness. Anthony had seen photographs of the garden. The garden was a marvellous sight of beauty. He wondered at it. He marvelled at it.

Joining Mrs Wills and his Mother. They had afternoon tea together. Thinking of Angelica. Anthony felt too upset, sad and miserable. He had been disappointed at Angelica not being present. Her absence upset Anthony. However, Anthony expected it. Angelica not coming to tea today. So he wasn't too disappointed!

Leaving his Mother and Mrs Wills to talk. Anthony sat out in the garden in the cool shade. There he fantasised. Dreaming of Angelica. Sitting on a garden chair. Cooling down in the shade. Anthony nodded off. Breathing in the fresh air.

Anthony dreamt of Angelica! Waking up in the garden. Anthony had fantasies of Angelica. Realising it was only a fantasy, a dream. He remained realistic and optimistic about Angelica.

Chapter 10

Daydreams

Anthony spent time studying in the Dining room. He sat at the Dining table while doing his studies. His Mother came into the Dining room. Mrs Dobbs disturbed her son doing his studies. Anthony took a break and rested.

"Did you like your tea? What did you think of BLUE ORCHID?" asked Mother.

"I had a lovely tea. BLUE ORCHID is a lovely place. It was disappointing Angelica didn't come to tea. I expected Angelica wouldn't come. Maybe it's because of me why she didn't come. I don't know the reason why? I like Angelica. She's a nice girl. A lady. She's popular. Her friends really like her. I wish I had friends like hers. I don't have hardly any friends. I am a loner. I am sad and lonely. I read and write. I enjoy gardening and listening to music. I do like to have tea in the garden with Mrs Wills and I enjoy going in the garden. It's so peaceful and quiet. It's such a beautiful garden. I look forward to coming to BLUE ORCHID. I dread not meeting Angelica. Angelica doesn't love me. She never will. I don't think I will ever see her much. Angelica is fascinating. She's strange."

"Angelica studying too. She has got her studies,"

reminded Mother.

"I dream of Angelica. My dreams never come true."

"Son. Get on with your studies. Never mind your girls," admonished Mother.

"Everyone is in love. Aren't they? Apart from me," moaned son.

"Get on with your work," said Mother sternly.

Mrs Dobbs left her son's untidy bedroom. Anthony tired of studying resumed doing his studies. Then finally after having enough of doing his studying. He stopped his studies and daydreamed.

The sun shone through the sash windows. The radiant sun was blazing.

He enjoyed his time daydreaming. He had romantic dreams and fantasies of Angelica!

Going to bed late that night. Anthony dreamt of Angelica. He had a beautiful dream of paradise!

There the playful children played in the garden. Anthony had such a happy time playing with Angelica. He had been beatific in the company of Angelica. Both playful children have great fun. It's a dream…

Chapter 11

Late Night Conversation

One night Anthony and Jane stayed up late and talked.

Anthony confided in his sister Jane. Jane was a good listener and a talker. Jane was sympathetically sweet towards her Brother. Understanding her Brother's disenchantment. His illusion was a pretence.

"Whenever I am invited to Mrs Wills for tea. Angelica never goes."

"Give her up. Angelica's not right for you," insisted Sister.

"If you say so," mumbled Brother.

"Mrs Wills discourages it, I take it."

"I haven't thought about it. I don't think Mrs Wills encourages it," said Brother. unsurely.

"Well. Whatever. You're not seeing Angelica. Really you are not."

"NO. I am not," answered Brother.

"Angelica's pampered. Isn't she? She's rich."

"I guess she is. I wish I could see her," wished Anthony.

"Don't get attached to Angelica. You mustn't."

"I shan't."

With impatience, Anthony left his sister in a downstairs room.

"Goodnight!" said Brother impatiently.

"Do say your prayers," urged Sister.

Anthony acknowledged his sister. Knowing about the importance of prayer. He has a spiritual sense of the experience of being prayerful.

"Sis. I will. Spooky!"

Anthony came out of the lounge. Going upstairs to his bedroom. In the dark bedroom. He got in bed. He fell fast asleep. That night he dreamt of the Garden of Love. It was a paradise dream!

Chapter 12

The Mid - Afternoon Walk Out in the Garden

During the mid-afternoon, Anthony came out into the garden. There he joined his Mother for a walk out in the garden. The spring weather had its natural freshness. The air was cool. The trees blossomed.

Anthony walked with his Mother around the garden.

"Having tea with Mrs Wills makes me bittersweet. Angelica is never there. Is she? What is she? A Ghost! She's not real."

"Mrs Aldridge has been dead for a century. What has happened to the generations? Nothing has changed, has it? They are far richer. The greedy prosper," said Mother disrespectfully.

"I don't see Angelica hardly anymore. She's never there! The woman is strange. They are all strange!" remarked Son.

"Not a word. Off with you. Go and tidy your room," ordered Mother.

Anthony disobeyed his Mother. He stayed out in the garden. In his mind he imagined Angelica. He pictured images in his mind. Realising it was a mental image, a figment of his imagination. He rejected the idea. He had lost hope in Angelica. His desire for her was a fantasy. Nonetheless, he thought of happier times with Angelica. His memories of her were good ones. His pleasant memory of Angelica made him deeply emotional.

Angelica came to tea. Then Angelica declined invitations to Mrs Wills' garden tea. Angelica was shunning Anthony on purpose.

He tolerated Angelica's ways. He had disrespect and disregard for Angelica.

The Grand-daughter was loved and highly regarded. Angelica's Mother protected her Daughter on the basis of discipline.

Mrs Dobbs and her son continued to have tea with Mrs Wills at BLUE ORCHID. They were good friends and they both remained loyal and patriotic.

Anthony felt disappointed at Angelica for not coming to tea today at Mrs Wills'. Angelica never came to tea whenever Mrs Dobbs and her Son were invited to BLUE ORCHID. Anthony wondered if he would ever see Angelica again.

Why didn't Angelica come to tea? What was the true reason for her absence? Did Angelica's Mother prevent her youngest Daughter from coming to tea? Angelica declined the invitation to tea. Thinking of it Anthony got deeply upset and disappointed in Angelica for not coming to garden tea at Mrs Wills'. Anthony probably would never see Angelica ever again! Was Angelica dead? Was she a ghost? The Ancestor bore a striking resemblance. Angelica was a Grand-Daughter look-alike. Her resemblance was a likeness!

In his dreams, Anthony dreamt of Angelica in the garden of love.

Going to tea at Mrs Wills' again. In the meantime, Anthony stayed in the country house downstairs when going in a room. Looking at the portraiture on the walls. He saw Ancestors throughout from the different generations. Anthony got confused by the sight of the portraiture. He stood and admired one portrait. A lovely portrait of Angelica? He marvelled at it. He was mournful and tearful.

Leaving the room. He then came out outside into the garden where he re-joined Mrs Wills and his Mother who was waiting for Anthony to come and join them for afternoon tea. Sitting down at the garden table. Anthony fantasised about Angelica. In his mind he pictured Angelica. He imagined Angelica being out here at Blue Orchid out in the garden. He fantasised about being alone with Angelica in the garden. He then soon realized it was only just a fantasy. His fantasies were not real at all. It was not even a reality. It was only just a dream!

One day at Blue Orchid in the garden. Sitting together in the shade. Mrs Wills showed Mrs Dobbs and her son old black and white photographs. To his great surprise, Anthony saw an old photograph of Angelica. With wonder, he spent time looking at it. A picture of an elegant Grand-daughter in a garden. In summertime this garden was beautiful. A dream garden.

One night. Anthony dreamt of Angelica in a beautiful garden. Coming closer, Anthony saw Angelica dressed in white, standing in the light. The shining light reflecting from her figure. ANTHONY going towards Angelica in the shadows. They smiled beatifically at each other. Their charm, a delight.

Anthony and Angelica held hands while walking together in the garden. The beatific romantic pair were deeply in love when walking together in the garden of love in the afterglow.

PART TWO

Chapter 1

Angelica's Surprise Visit

(Stately Prominence)

Anthony and his Mother accepted an invitation to tea at Blue Orchid with Mrs Wills and her Grand-daughter. Anthony was pleased with the invitation. He was pleasantly surprised that Angelica had come to tea. (Usually, Angelica was always absent whenever Anthony and his Mother came to tea.)

Anthony, his Mother, Mrs Wills and her Grand-daughter sat at the garden table outside in the garden. They ate tea on a lovely hot summer's day.

Feeling hot, sweaty and dehydrated in the heat, Angelica helped herself to cordial from a glass jug. She poured out some cordial for Anthony who reached out to pass his glass to Angelica. Angelica thoughtfully poured a jugful of cordial into his glass. Anthony feeling thirsty gulped it down. He spilt some on his shirt.

Mrs Wills and Anthony's Mother talked away to their hearts' content. Becoming bored with their conversation both Anthony and Angelica asked to be excused. They had been polite and well-mannered when getting up and leaving the garden table. They both walked in the direction of the house a short way away.

"You don't like me," said Anthony.

"Like you? Why would I have come, if I didn't like you," expostulated Angelica.

Anthony took umbrage. He protested. Showing some defiance in a loud tone of voice, he raised an objection,

"Why on earth bother coming!"

"Pipe down! I am here now," gestured Angelica.

Angelica and Anthony went back indoors. Anthony followed Angelica who led him into a large room. This furnished room was spacious with a suite in it. Also in it were antiques and hanging on all four walls were portraiture and paintings. Standing opposite a portrait, Angelica proudly pointed at it. Her gestures were ladylike and graceful. She was beautiful and dressed up. Angelica was elegant and an attention-seeker.

"This one is my Great Grandmother."

"It is. Is it?" stared Anthony.

"Yeah, it is. A lady."

Anthony stood next to Angelica who was pointing at it. He felt overwhelmed as well as lost in fascination. Marvelling at the uncanny strangeness of it. The portrait of an Ancestor, Angelica's Great Grandmother.

"You look like your Grandmother," said Anthony assuredly.

Angelica put her hands on her hips.

"Do you think so?"

"Yes. You do. Isn't that a coincidence?"

Angelica with joy took pride.

"It runs in the family," smiled Angelica.

"Tell me about your Great Grandmother," enquired Anthony.

Angelica unresponded with a response. Anthony tried to prompt a response from Angelica.

"Tell me something. Anything about your Great Grandmother."

"I can't say. Well, my Great Grandmother was a Lady. She married a nobleman, a landowner. She had a daughter. She lived in an estate. Her dream was to live in a palace in a lovely garden. She fulfilled her dream. That was owning a dream garden. She used to love gardening and entertaining," answered Angelica.

Anthony dwelt on the heritage.

"Oh! How nice. That's interesting. It's grand and historic. The estate with gardens. Then handed down to the generations. The estate preserved," exclaimed Anthony matter-of-factly.

"You see, it's held in a trust," mentioned Angelica.

"Oh! It is. Isn't that remarkable? How imposing it must be."

"It is. It's a dream," sighed Angelica.

With curious fascination, Anthony did wonder.

"Do you like to look like her?"

With pretence, Angelica acted like a princess with airs and graces.

"I am so used to it. I haven't thought about it. I just take it for granted as usual. I am a Lady. So bow down to me," commanded Angelica.

Angelica stretched out her hand and made a demand.

Anthony revered Angelica. He had an afterthought. He obeyed Angelica. A stately figure. He moved forward to bow down in her presence.

Angelica reacted to Anthony's initial reaction. Angelica with grace made a curtsy.

"You see that wasn't hard," gestured Angelica.

"You must do that to everyone," motioned Anthony.

"Oh! I do. I am a Lady! I am a Queen. A Princess too," blustered Angelica.

In disbelief, Anthony admired Angelica. Of course, he had a deep revere for her. Of the deepest adoration and admiration for her.

Angelica stood and fanned herself. She cooled down. Angelica perspired from the blazing sunrays shining through the large windows. Perspiring in the heat. Angelica was dazed. In a daze, she walked into a chair. Her airs and graces were stately. Angelica's sapphire diamond ring sparkled. Angelica made a gesture. Followed by clapping her hands.

"NOW GO! Leave me!" urged Angelica.

Anthony obeyed Angelica's command. He knew Angelica was difficult and temperamental. At once he left her all alone. He would like to see her again if the opportunity arose.

Going outdoors Anthony joined Mrs Wills and her Mother in the garden. With anticipation of departure. At present both son and Mother departed. They had both overstayed their welcome. Appreciating Mrs Wills' invite.

Angelica avoided them. Angelica, conceited, haughty, disrespectful and unsociable did not say goodbye to either of them as they left Blue Orchid to make their journey home.

Anthony remembered the day. It remained a good memory.

Anthony hoped he would see Angelica again. He knew for certain Mrs Wills would invite him and his Mother to Blue Orchid again quite soon. The invitation was compliments of Mrs Wills.

Anthony wondered if he would meet Angelica there again.

Perhaps Angelica would consider declining the invitation this time with Mrs Wills, her Aunt?

Angelica was avoiding Anthony, a deliberate intention and motive of hers!

Chapter 2

Anthony's Deep Reflection on Angelica

Anthony's Mother came into the Living Room. The parent brought in a tray and put it on the table. They both sat down on the settee and had a nice cup of tea together. They refreshed from drinking tea. They both felt satisfied at the pleasure of drinking tea. It was a pleasurable enjoyment.

"How did you find it?" asked Mother.

"Oh! It was good. Mrs Wills is awfully nice and kind. I do like going there. Really, I do. I can't wait to go there again," said Anthony excitedly.

"And Angelica?" murmured Mother.

Anthony deeply reflected on Angelica.

"I don't know what to say about her. Angelica is nice. Other times she's awful. She's here one minute. Then gone. Then she doesn't come. That's her," frowned Anthony.

"Angelica a Lady. Do be nice to her," admonished Mother.

Anthony confirmed his intention.

"Oh! I will be nice to her. Angelica has vibes. She has that aura."

"Mrs Wills likes you."

"Does she? I am glad Mrs Wills approves of me. Mrs Wills is a lovely woman. So sweet and nice," complimented Son.

"Yes. Anything else you want to say?"

"That portrait of Angelica's Ancestor is strange and odd. It really is Blue Orchid. Isn't it? There's no doubt about it. It's centuries old. Is it haunted? Is it a blessing!" added Son.

"I should think so. It runs in the family for generations," remarked Mother.

"Aren't the other paintings and portraits taken down?"

The Mother spoke about something unclear and ambiguous.

"That one stands the test of time. How strange it is," said Mother ambiguously.

"Do you mean the portrait? It is remarkable," exclaimed Son.

"That portrait is the essence of Blue Orchid. There's no doubt about it."

"Yeah, I agree with you," nodded Son.

The Mother confirmed the rearranged portrait.

"Next to it is a portrait of Angelica."

The Son was confused at the rearrangement of portraiture.

"Is it really?" puzzled Son.

"Oh! It is," confirmed Mother.

Anthony pictured a mystic image in his mind. The portraiture. The mystical imagery of a dark background. A shadowy light and shadow.

Angelica and her Great Grandmother had a resemblance, a likeness of identical twins.

Anthony had taken note of the resemblance.

"Oh! How strange. They both do look alike. There's a change to the layout. A portrait put in a new place," remembered Anthony.

"Ahem! Family reasons. Family sentimentality," snorted Mother.

Anthony remembered the portraiture and miscellaneous art with the contemporary respectively. He thought it must be a typical family trait of theirs. (They are art collectors and antique dealers.)

Anthony shuddered. He took discomfort from his seated position. The room temperature dropped.

Late at night, Anthony got up from the armchair. He stood up and stretched his legs.

"Goodnight," said Son snortingly.

Anthony left his Mother alone downstairs. Anthony went to bed late that night. Anthony dreamt of Angelica. A sweet dream!

A few nights ago he had a bad nightmare!

Chapter 3

Christmas Break

Coming back from the snowy Alps. Both Mother and Son entered the cosy log cabin. They took comfort from being warmed up. They indulged in comfort. They sat together. It was a loving relationship between Son and Mother. They were both enthralled by the Christmas spirit. They took joy at Christmas. (Anthony's Mother was an Employee of a Tour Operator and treated her son to a seasonal break at Christmas.)

Both Son and Mother enjoyed precious time together. His Mother was peaceable, merry, joyful and happy at Christmastime. At this seasonal time, they both felt peaceful, overjoyed and excited about Christmas. They stayed at a chalet near the Austrian Alps. The mountainous Alps near where there was an avalanche.

Anthony thought of Angelica. Anthony wanted some sympathy. He felt sorry for himself.

"Angelica doesn't love me," said Son.

"Oh! But she does. She wouldn't invite you. Would she?" hummed Mother.

Anthony's answer was emphatic.

"I guess not," said Son laconically.

"Mrs Wills likes you very much," smiled Mother.

"Oh! Does she really? I think she does. Mrs Wills wouldn't invite me if she didn't."

"At least Angelica makes the effort to see you," said Mother.

"Well, she does. It's better than nothing," uttered Son.

They both stayed together. Keeping warm inside. The heat insulated.

They took the opportunity to spend time together. An electrifying Christmas in a chalet near the Austrian Alps. It was a seasonal beautiful Christmas.

They wished each other a Happy Christmas and a Merry Christmas.

Chapter 4

Anthony's Brief Time Alone at Blue Orchid

Standing and looking at the portraiture, Anthony wondered if it had been removed and replaced.

He was puzzled at all the different positions and places. (There were more and more reproductions which had been hung up as a result of favourable preference.)

With eager interest, Anthony stood and admired all of the oil paintings. He took a look at the portraiture. He thought the portraiture was of Ancestors from the past generations. The most common ones were unusual portraits of both Mrs Wills' Great Grandmother and Angelica her Grand-daughter. Standing still with his mouth agape. He wondered if the portrait of the Great Grandmother was haunting. He tried to discern if Blue Orchid was haunted. It was of spontaneity. He overreacted. Perhaps it was a spontaneous overreaction. He imagined it!

The house-proud host reassured Anthony. A Priest blessed Blue Orchid by giving it a blessing! (At other premises a housewarming house party had been held.)

Anthony must have seen these several times by now. He had forgotten how many times he kept seeing the portraiture.

He wandered somewhere else. He adventured into a sitting room. To his unsurprise he saw in there a fine collection of dolls everywhere around the spacious sitting room. It was furnished and luxurious. He wondered if they belong to Angelica.

He saw many dolls. (Anthony already knew a few names of the dolls. He remembered the names of the dolls which Angelica called them. Angelica briefly mentioned it to him in a girlish playful way. Angelica was overwhelmed with excitement.)

Anthony looked at Rhoda, a cowgirl, Jeanette, a French fashion model doll, and Squark, a beefy commander with a gun.

Suddenly Mrs Wills entered the sitting room. Mrs Wills intruded on Anthony who was looking around the room with curious interest.

"Do you like them? They are my Grand-daughter's," pointed out Mrs Wills.

Anthony liked the dolls. He approved of the doll collection.

"Oh! Yes. They are lovely dolls. I see Angelica collects dolls. They are nice ones. They are in good condition," answered Anthony.

"Angelica loves dolls. She collects them. The dog chewed one up. The eye fell out of it," smirked Mrs Wills.

"Oh! What a pity," laughed Anthony.

Both Anthony and Mrs Wills went outdoors. They both joined Anthony's Mother sitting out in the garden at the garden table. Together, the few of them had tea out in the lovely garden in summer. Angelica didn't come today. Again, she declined the invitation to have tea with her Aunt and invited welcomed guests at Blue Orchid. This time Angelica refused to come. Attending music practice instead.

Anthony missed Angelica. He was too upset at her absence. With total unsurprise he had expected Angelica not to come to tea today. He liked Angelica. He was fond of her. He was deeply attracted to her in a sentimental way. Anthony greatly missed Angelica. He felt badly upset. He simply just coped without her. Feeling upset, he tried to be cheerful, polite and nice. He was on his best behaviour and wore his best clothes.

He found out that he had been disappointed again. He got hurt from disappointment. He stayed calm and cool despite being deeply upset again. Anthony was deeply contemplative and reflective. He stayed quiet whilst Mrs Wills and his Mother talked away.

Anthony became bored at unlistening to their conversation. Anthony asked to be excused. He got up and left the garden table. He walked down the garden.

The Garden of Love

There he came to a few garden chairs somewhere in the garden. He sat down on a chair. He stayed seated. He deeply reflected on the absence of Angelica. He badly missed Angelica. He was tearful and in an unhappy mood. He wanted to cry. He suppressed his tears. Sitting out alone in the garden. He dozed off. The breezy air felt fresh and cool in the shade. The heat was sultry.

He enjoyed the peace and quiet and quietude relaxing alone in a shady spot. Anthony stayed by himself for some time in deep meditation.

About a few hours later, at home, Anthony took the time to talk to his Mother about Angelica. His Mother remained indifferent to her son's deep concern for Angelica. Anthony grumbled about Angelica. At making a point on a re-cap.

"Angelica is never here. Is she? Why does she bother? She isn't here. Why does she bother to come? She shouldn't come," tutted Son.

The Mother stick up for Angelica.

"Angelica has got her life to live. Hasn't she? She does have commitments. You ought to understand that," said Mother firmly.

"Oh, I do. Angelica has responsibilities. Why on earth did I bother to meet her!" grumbled Son.

"Dear! Angelica is a Lady. What does she have to meet you for? She doesn't have to see you at all," defended Mother.

The Son was provoked by his Mother's unprovocative response. He kept calm and cool. He sat in a comfortable seated position. With both his hands clasped together. With undoubt Anthony agreed (on condition of decency).

"You're right. Why should she come? Angelica's a princess!"

Anthony felt humiliated from embarrassment as well as disappointment. He felt too hurt, unhappy, frustrated and miserable. He still kept his dignity, despite his deep miseries, dissatisfaction and discontentment.

Chapter 5

The Derby

Today, they went to the Derby which was a main race schedule. Anthony joined Mrs Wills and her Grand-daughter and her Mother in a stand. Standing up, Angelica looked through binoculars as she watched the jockeys on their racehorses riding to the finishing line. The others looked on and cheered. The previous race ended up as a photo finish.

Finally, after the last race of the day ended, Anthony joined Mrs Wills and her Grand-daughter who accompanied them away from the racecourse and boundaries where they found a professional jockey sitting on a racehorse waiting for them. There also amongst the entourage were elegant and chic Ladies of Cheltenham.

With favour, Anthony appreciated his privilege. He had been privileged to have a day out at the races.

Angelica loved horses. She was a good rider. An enthusiast. Mrs Wills' Husband was a Steward by occupation. Angelica's Uncle had a passion for racehorses.

Anthony was overwhelmed by the Ladies' presence. Anthony got the chance to meet all the elegant and chic women dressed up in lovely hats, gloves, scarves, accessories and separates.

Anthony saw them unexpectedly. He swooned at the sight of them. He ogled them standing together on a boundary. They all took his breath away. He marvelled at the fine, fair beauties and also the other Englishwomen's good looks.

Anthony experienced something new and unusual. He became experienced at meeting the jet set and elite too. He enjoyed himself. The day out at the races was memorable.

Due to security restrictions, Mrs Wills and her lovely Grand-daughter had left to set off on their journey home.

Both Anthony and his Mother stayed at a hotel overnight before leaving to commute back to London.

Returning home. All alone Anthony reflected on his unforgettable day out at the races. This Derby lived up to expectations. The race itself was exciting.

Anthony and Mrs Wills Watch a Cricket Match

Anthony and Mrs Wills went to a local cricket match at a cricket ground. From the stand, they both enjoyed watching the County Cricket.

It was a good one-day cricket match with a certain number of overs delivered.

Barnsley the Batsman's innings was fifty not out.

Eventually, his team won by four wickets, innings.

Anthony got to know Mr Wills well. Mr Wills has a passion for cricket. His son Barnaby-Croft had an interest in cricket too.

Angelica disliked cricket. She found it a rather boring sport.

Chapter 6

Midnight Love in the Garden

Anthony attended the party with his Mother at Blue Orchid. He came to this place frequently with his Mother to visit Mrs Wills.

Angelica was regarded as the Host as it was her Birthday. Angelica remained popular amongst the guests. They all showered Angelica with Birthday presents. She may have been adored and admired by every guest invited to Angelica's party. They found her lovable and adorable. Angelica possessed a sweet nature. Attracting attention as she was comely and personable.

Anthony, an invited guest, felt at ease at Blue Orchid as he was used to coming here. He charmed at Blue Orchid. The home sweet home. It was a delightful sweet notion!

Everybody wanted Angelica's attention. She remained popular among all of the guests. They all liked her. She was deemed the most likeable person. They respected and revered her. They had a high regard for Angelica. The guests followed her around, wanting her company. Her friendship. Desiring her and seeking her attention.

Going into the dining room, they had a repast. Everyone helped themselves to party food. Then the guests danced in the ballroom where there were French windows and a balcony.

Meeting Angelica in the drawing room, Anthony came up and spoke to her. He was indifferent, shy and self-conscious. He suffered from an inferiority complex. Thinking others were superior to him. Of course, they had a high status. He didn't bother talking to any of them. From first impressions they were strangers. They may be snobs, upper middle class, upper crust or Aristocrats.

"You're high class," remarked Anthony.

"You're not bad yourself."

Anthony spoke in an upper-middle-class accent. He tried to do a posh voice. He tried to impress Angelica who seemed quite impressed by his upper-crust voice and accent. So posh!

"My Lady! Pleased to serve you as always. Join me," said Anthony affectedly.

Other posh guests looked on. They objected to Anthony being invited to Blue Orchid. From being given an invitation to Angelica's birthday party. A high priority. They disapproved of him. A sense of disapproval! Anthony found favour with Angelica. Angelica disapproved of him.

That summer night Anthony didn't dance. He could not dance.

Angelica decided to dance with her friends. Angelica impressed everyone with her dancing. Angelica was good at dancing.

During that time in the ballroom, Anthony was humiliated, embarrassed and frustrated. Anthony stayed alone by himself. Feeling lonely he kept away from everybody else. He eluded them, intent on eating a sandwich wrapped up in a napkin. Anthony felt enervated and tired. He took the time to rest himself. He recovered.

Anthony got the surprise of his life when Angelica came to him late that night. In the presence of guests. Angelica took hold of his arm and held him tightly. They both walked together through the house and garden. Along the way passing by guests.

Anthony felt deeply beatific. He was overwhelmed with a deep love for Angelica. Gathered outside, all of the guests looked at them. Anthony smiled with joy. He was filled with beatitude. At this time, he felt so blissful! He had never felt this way in all of his life before. Tonight, was a great exception!

There was such great love. There was love in the air. All the merry and joyous guests celebrated Angelica's birthday.

All the merry-makers raised their glasses and made a toast to Angelica who declared her love to them.

"What can I say? This is a great night for me. One I shall cherish forever. Thank you all for coming to my birthday. I love you so much. I love you, Anthony.

Anthony, you are a dream. If it was not for you, I would have no dream at all. You've made my dream come true. In this garden tonight," said Angelica beatifically.

Both Anthony and Angelica walked arm in arm together around the beautiful garden. In the bright shining garden lights. Both of them could clearly see the guests' natural expressions of love and joy. Appreciating their deep love and affection. They both cherished their time in a paradise garden of love at midnight.

- The End -

*Available worldwide from Amazon
and all good bookstores*

Michael Terence Publishing

www.mtp.agency

www.facebook.com/mtp.agency

@mtp_agency